The Tailor's Gift

A Holiday Tale for Everyone

by David M. Stern

illustrated by Dave Zaboski

Special acknowledgements to Roberto Blain for helping me manifest my vision;

Peggi Garvey for her creative input and unyielding dedication in helping me to create the right words;

Matheu Brooks for layout and design; Joseph Amster and Sarika Chawla for their help with editing;

and, as always, to my wonderful family for their continuous love and support.

DP

Doc's Productions, Inc.

Los Angeles, CA

Doc's Productions, Inc.

8235 Santa Monica Blvd., suite 306

Los Angeles, CA 90046

First Printing, September 2005

for Rachel

It was bedtime in the pasture

and the stars were dancing with the moon.

The lambs were restless

as Mamma and Papa tried to settle them down to sleep.

Close your eyes and go to dreamland," said Mamma.

"We can't," moaned the lambs.

"Have you tried counting people?" asked Papa.

"Oh Papa, that never works. Tell us a story pleeease!" they cried.

"All right, all right," calmed Mamma. "But just one."

Once

upon

a long,

long,

time ago…

*H*igh upon a mountain meadow,

lived a tailor with his flock of sheep.

*T*he tailor was a kind man

with a very fine eye.

His name was Shimmel Cloth

and his sheep were well fed and happy.

They grew the thickest wool that made the warmest clothes.

*S*himmel Cloth was full of love and always had an encouraging word.

The villagers felt that love and knew they would be bundled in warmth when the winter came.

Each time the villagers climbed up the mountain, Shimmel Cloth thanked them and said,

"If there is ever anything I can do for you, I promise, I will."

The villagers always replied,

"All you need to do is make us fine garments and treat us fairly."

And he did.

*E*veryone lived happily in the village,

until one winter the North Wind decided to blow his coldest ice and snow

down the mountain.

"We're chilled to the bone," shivered the people.

"My fireplace can't keep my house warm.

What am I going to do?" worried a mother.

"What are we all going to do?" others chimed in.

They decided to join together,

so they gathered all the wood they could carry

and brought it to the inn at the edge of town.

*T*ogether they built the biggest fire anyone had ever seen.

As the light filled the room everyone felt safe and warm again.

They made a delicious stew, and later,

the children snuggled and were told bedtime stories.

Finally, everyone rested with the fire burning bright.

While they were sleeping,

the bitter North Wind came down

with a **thundering blow!**

In the blink of an eye,

the North Wind picked up the embers of

the fire and scattered them throughout

the town.

*B*efore anyone knew it,

the whole town was ablaze,

burning out of control.

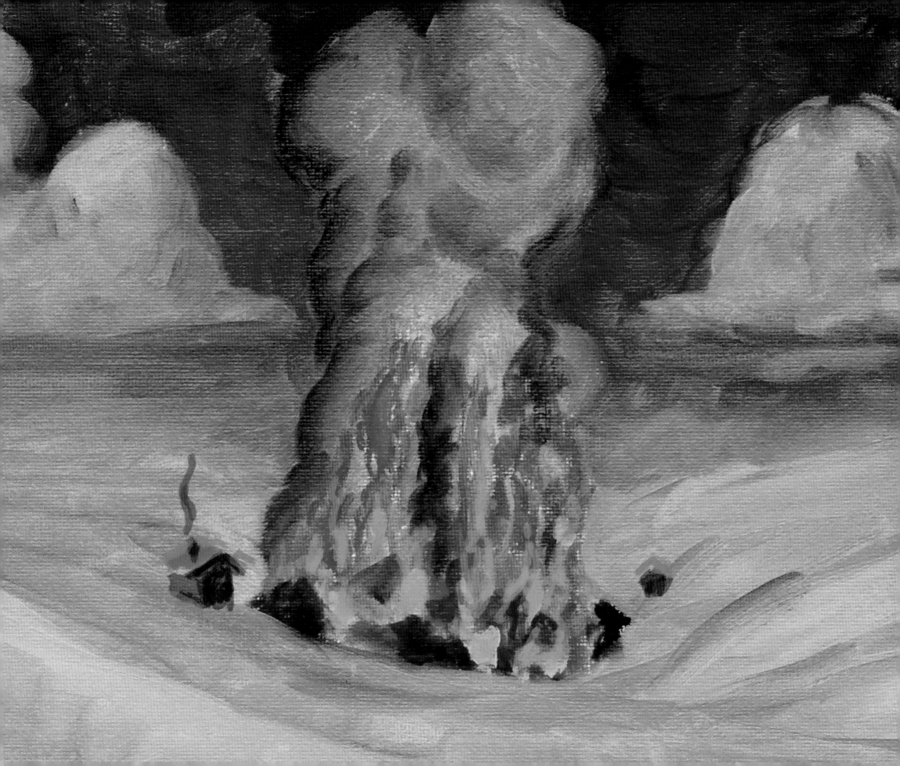

$\mathcal{F}$ire! Fire!" panicked a baby lamb, tugging on his mother.

"Oh No!" screamed the flock. "Shimmel, come quickly! The town is burning."

Seeing the fire, Shimmel Cloth remembered his words: "If there's ever anything I can do for you, I promise I will."

"We must help them!" he declared.

*S*himmel Cloth and his helpers gathered all the clothes they had made.

They stuffed coats, hats, sweaters, scarves, shirts and socks

into large sacks and piled them high onto the sled.

"Let us help," offered the sheep.

"We can pull the sled."

One sheep shouted out,

"You can have the wool off our backs!"

With knitting needles and scissors hung around their necks

to make more clothes for the villagers,

the sheep began to pull the sled down the snowy mountain.

We must hurry, but the slopes are slippery and the roads can be rough.

Be careful," warned Shimmel Cloth.

"Don't worry, Shimmel. We'll be fine," replied the sheep.

Shimmel and his flock hit

bump after bump

on their journey until they stumbled

and went tumbling through the air.

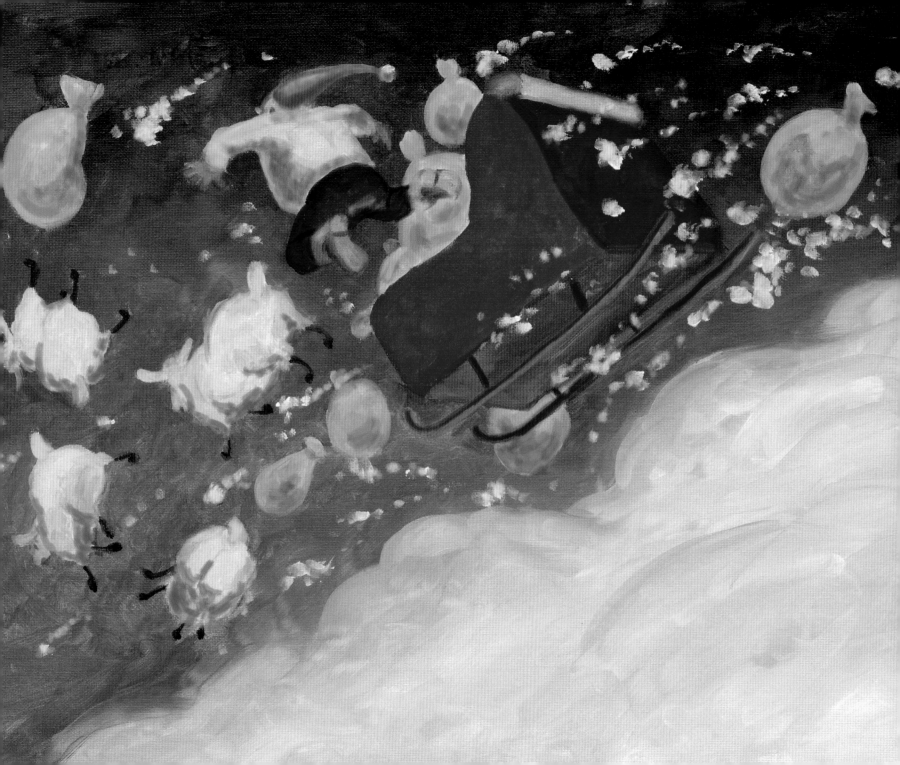

*T*hey landed with a splat!

The clothes flew everywhere.

"Baaah Humbug!" groaned the sheep.

"I'm too cold."

"I'm too wet."

"I'm too sore."

"This is too hard!"

"The road is bumpy and we've just had enough!"
they complained as their teeth chattered, echoing off the mountain.

W hen the road is bumpy and you've just had enough, look inside yourself

and make yourself tough," Shimmel replied.

"It's all in how you look at things. Are we going to let the bitter North Wind

and a couple of bumps in the road stop us?

We can use them to help us!"

Even though the sheep didn't quite know what Shimmel Cloth meant,

they trusted him.

So they shook off the cold and their fear and continued down the mountain.

*F*rom that point on,

with every bump,

they tried a little harder and grew a little stronger.

Nothing stopped them.

"Yippee," the sheep shouted gleefully.

"There's another bump ahead,"

Shimmel pointed.

"Go over it! Go over it!"

"Wheeee!" cheered the sheep.

"Let's fly!"

(These are the first moguls in recorded history.)

The village burned until there was

nothing left but embers and ashes.

Everyone sighed with sadness

except one little boy

who turned to look

at the beauty of the sunrise.

He could not believe what he saw.

What's that?" asked the child.

"Who's that?" wondered the villagers.

W hy, it's Shimmel Cloth. What are you doing here?" they asked.

"Can't you see we have nothing left, and we can't buy your beautiful clothes?"

"What do you mean you have nothing left?"
Shimmel questioned. "Just look around you."

Everyone looked around and then back at Shimmel Cloth.

"We have nothing!" they cried.

"Look very carefully at what's right next to you,"
Shimmel pointed to a man in the crowd,
"and what's right next to you," he pointed to another,
"and what's next to you, and you, and you," he motioned to them all.
"You still have what's most important.
You have each other," Shimmel reminded them.
"And you have me."

$\mathcal{A}$t that moment a ray of hope shined down upon the village.

Together

they handed out the clothes that Shimmel and

his sheep had brought down the mountain and

together

they worked until the village thrived once again.

nd so the story has been told down through the ages. It was Shimmel

Cloth, the tailor, who taught us the true spirit of giving," Mamma sheep told

her lambs as they drifted onto dreamland.

*T*he same spirit of giving lives in all of us.

Be kind to each other

And

Live in Peace

Not the end, a new beginning

Tips for Helping Children Learn the Spirit of Giving During the Holiday Season

- Ask children how they think they can help others in need.

- Have the children name three of their toys or books they would be willing to give to children with less.

- If your community has an Angel Tree or similar way to give to those in need, plan a trip to donate or select the name of a needy child.

- Discuss how giving to others makes them feel.

- Send holiday gifts to an organization that will distribute them to children in need.

- Make of list of friends and family they want to give gifts to, and see if there is something they can make (rather than buy) or do for each of these people.

- Send holiday cards or letters to men and women serving overseas.

About the Author

David M. Stern is the co-founder and publisher of IN Los Angeles Magazine. He is a screenwriter, journalist, lyricist, and poet. David has been versed in the art of story telling since he learned how to talk. He lives nestled in a historically protected area of the Hollywood Hills where the energy of the bygone era of old Hollywood nourishes his creative aspirations daily. His niece Rachel inspired "The Tailor's Gift."

About the Illustrator

Dave Zaboski was an animator for Disney Studios during the last golden period of animation. His credits include "Beauty and the Beast," "Aladdin," "Pocahontas," "Fantasia 2000," and at least seven other classic films. His paintings, portraits and drawings have been shown internationally. He teaches workshops and classes in the creative process and lives with his wife Robin and daughter Grace on a small ranch in Chatsworth, California.

Questions courtesy of KSB Promotions